I See Summer

by Charles Ghigna

illustrated by Ag Jatkowska

PICTURE WINDOW BOOKS

a capstone imprint

I see sunshine when I wake.

I see families at the lake.

I see sailboats passing by.

I see seagulls in the sky.

I see rain coats and rain showers.

I see gardens full of flowers.

I see trails of snails and slugs.

I see lots of ladybugs.

I see seesaws in the shade.

I see homemade lemonade.

I see swimsuits at the store.

I see seashells at the shore.

I see minnows in the creek.

I see games of hide-n-seek.

I see people without shoes.

I see backyard barbecues.

I see ice cream in a cone.

I see a puppy with a bone.

I see picnics in the park.

I see fireflies at dark.

The End

—for Charlotte and Christopher

I See is published by Picture Window Books
A Capstone Imprint
151 Good Counsel Drive, P.O. Box 669
Mankato, Minnesota 56002
www.capstonepub.com

Library of Congress Cataloging-in-Publication Data
Ghigna, Charles.
    I see summer / by Charles Ghigna ; illustrated by Ag Jatkowska.
        p. cm.
    Summary: Illustrations and easy-to-read, rhyming text show what makes summer special,
from sunshine and sailboats to ice cream and picnics.
ISBN 978-1-4048-6590-7 (library binding)
ISBN 978-1-4048-6852-6 (pbk.)
    [1. Stories in rhyme. 2. Summer--Fiction.] I. Jatkowska, Ag, ill. II. Title.
    PZ8.3.G345Ias 2011
    [E]--dc22
                                            2010050088

Creative Director: Heather Kindseth

Designer: Emily Harris

Printed in the United States of America in North Mankato, Minnesota.
032011
006110CGF11

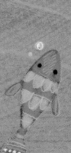